BY P

I

JEAN-BAPTISTE SIMÉON CHARDIN occupies a curious position among the artists of his time and country. His art which, neglected and despised for many decades after his death, is now admitted by those best competent to judge to be supreme as regards technical excellence,[10] and, within the narrow limits of its subject matter, to possess merits of far greater significance than are to be found in the work of any Frenchman, save Watteau, from the founding of the school of Fontainebleau to modern days, is apt to be regarded as an isolated phenomenon, un-French, out of touch, and out of sympathy with the expression of the artistic genius of eighteenth-century France. A grave misconception of the true inwardness of things! Rather should it be said that Chardin was the one typically French painter among a vast crowd of more or less close followers of a tradition imported from Italy; the one painter of the actual life of his people among the artificial caterers for an artificial and often depraved and lascivious taste; a man of the people, of the vast multitude formed by a homely, simple bourgeoisie; painting for the people the subjects that appealed to the people.

In order to understand the position of Chardin in the art of his country it is[11] necessary to bear in mind that the autochthonous painting of France, the real expression of French genius, was from its early beginnings closely connected with the art of the North, and not with that of Italy. The style of the early French miniaturists of the Burgundian School, of Fouquet and of Clouet, is the style of the North; their art is interwoven with the art of Flanders. When in the time of François I. the School of Fontainebleau, headed by Primaticcio and Rosso, promulgated the gospel that artistic salvation could only be found in the emulation of Raphael and the masters of the late Italian Renaissance, and of the Bolognese eclectics; when finally degenerated painters like Albani were held up as example, official art became altogether Italianised and stereotyped; and the climax was reached with the foundation of the School of Rome by Louis XIV. But, though officially neglected and looked upon with disfavour, the national element was not to be altogether crushed by the foreign importation.[12] Poussin remained French in spite of Italian training, and held aloof from the coterie of Court painters. Jacques Callot carried on the national tradition, though as a satirist and etcher of scenes from contemporary life, rather than as a painter. And the Netherlands continued directly or indirectly to stir up the sluggish stream of national French art—directly through Watteau, who, born a Netherlander, became the most typically French of all French painters; indirectly, half a century earlier, through the brothers Le Nain, who drew their subjects and inspiration from the North and their sombre colour from Spain; and afterwards through Chardin, whose style was so closely akin to that of the Flemings that, when he first submitted some pieces of still-life to the members of the Academy, Largillière himself took them to be the work of some excellent unknown Flemish painter.

What are the qualities that raise Chardin's art so high above the showy productions[14] of the French painters of his generation, placing him on a pedestal by himself, and gaining for him the respect, the admiration, the love of all artists and discerning art lovers? Why should this painter of still-life and of small unpretentious domestic genre pieces be extolled without reservation and ranked among the world's greatest masters?

PLATE II.—LA FONTAINE (THE WOMAN DRAWING WATER)
(In the National Gallery, London)

"La Fontaine," or the "Woman Drawing Water," is one of the two examples of Chardin's art in the National Gallery. It is the subject of which probably most versions are in existence, and figured among the eight pictures sent by the master to the Salon of 1737, the first exhibition held since 1704, and the first in which Chardin appeared as a painter of genre pictures.

The original version, which bears the date 1733, is at the Stockholm Museum, and other replicas belong to Sir Frederick Cook in Richmond, M. Marcille in Paris, Baron Schwiter, and to the Louvre. The picture was engraved by Cochin.

The question finds its simplest solution in the fact that all great and lasting art must be based on the study of Nature and of contemporary life; that erudition and the imitation of the virtues of painters that belong to a dead period never result in permanent appeal, especially if they find expression in the repetition of mythological and allegorical formulas which belong to the past, and have long ceased to be a living language. Chardin's art is living and sincere, with never a trace of affectation. In his paintings the most unpromising material, the most prosaic objects on a humble kitchen table, the uneventful daily routine of lower[16] middle-class life, are rendered interesting by the warming flame of human sympathy which moved the master to spend his supreme skill upon them; by the human interest with which he knew how to invest even inanimate objects. No painter knew like Chardin how to express in terms of paint the substance and surface and texture of the most varied objects; few have ever equalled him in the faultless precision of his colour values; fewer still have carried the study of reflections to so fine a point, and observed with such accuracy the most subtle nuances of the changes wrought in the colour appearance of one object by the proximity of another—but these are qualities that only an artist can fully appreciate, and that can only be vaguely felt by the layman. They belong to the sphere of technique. The strong appeal of Chardin's still-life is due to the manner in which he invests inanimate objects with living interest, with a sense of intimacy that enlists our sympathy for the humble folk with whose existence[17] these objects are connected, and who, by mere accident as it were, just happen to be without the frame of the picture. Perhaps they have just left the room, but the atmosphere is still filled with their presence.

If ever there was a painter to whom the old saying *celare artem est summa ars* is applicable, surely it was Chardin! A slow, meticulously careful worker, who bestowed no end of time and trouble upon every canvas, and whom nothing but perfection would satisfy, he never attempted to gain applause by a display of cleverness or by technical fireworks. The perfection of the result conceals the labour expended upon it and the art by means of which it is achieved. And so it is with the composition. His still-life arrangements, where everything is deliberate selection, have an appearance of accidental grouping as though the artist, fascinated by the colour of some viands and utensils on a kitchen table, had yielded to an irresistible impulse, and forthwith painted the things just as they offered[18] themselves to his delighted vision. How different it all is to the conception of still-life of his compatriots of the "grand century" and even of his own time! It was a sad misconception of the function and range of art that made the seventeenth century draw the distinction between "noble" and "ignoble" subjects. When they "stooped" to still-life it had to be ennobled—that is to say, precious stuffs, elegant furniture, bronzes and gold or silver goblets, choice specimens of hot-house flowers, and such like material were piled up in what was considered picturesque abundance—and the whole thing was as theatrical and tasteless and sham-heroic as a portrait by Lebrun, the Court favourite. Even the Dutch and Flemish still-life painters of the period, who had a far keener appreciation of Nature, catered for the taste that preferred the display of riches to simple truth. Their flowers and fruit were carefully chosen faultless specimens, accompanied generally by costly objects and stuffs; and on the whole these[19] large decorative pieces were painted with wonderful accuracy in the rendering of each individual blossom or other detail, but with utter disregard of atmosphere. It has been rightly said that these

Netherlanders gave the same *kind* of attention to every object, whilst Chardin bestowed upon the component parts of his still-life compositions not the same kind, but the same *degree* of attention. And above all, whilst suggesting the texture and volume and material of each individual object with faultless accuracy, Chardin never lost sight of the ensemble—that is to say, the opposition of values, the interchange that takes place between the colours of two different objects placed in close proximity, the reflections which appear not only where they would naturally be expected, as on shiny copper or other metals, but even those on comparatively dull surfaces, which would probably escape the attention of the untrained eye. Chardin looked upon everything with a true painter's vision; and his[20] brush expressed not his knowledge of the form of things, but the visual impression produced by their ensemble. He did not think in outline, but in colour. If proof were needed, it will be found in the extreme scarcity of sketches and drawings from his hand. Only very few sketches by Chardin are known, and these few proclaim the painter rather than the draughtsman.

Still, having pointed out the gulf that divides our master from the still-life painters of the *grand siècle*, it is only right to add that he did not burst upon the world as an isolated phenomenon, and that painters like Desportes and Oudry form the bridge from Monnoyer, the best known of the French seventeenth-century compilers of showy monumental still-life, to Chardin. Monnoyer belongs to a time that knew neither respect nor genuine love for Nature and her laws. He simply followed the rules of the grand style, and had no eye for the play of reflections and the other problems, which are the delight[21] of the moderns— and Chardin is essentially modern. Monnoyer's son Baptiste, and his son-in-law Belin de Fontenay did not depart from his artificial manner. But with Oudry, in spite of much that is still traditional in his art, we arrive already at a new conception of still-life painting. In a paper read by this artist to the Academy he relates how, in his student days, when asked by Largillière to paint some flowers, he placed a carefully chosen, gaily coloured bouquet in a vase, when his master stopped him and said: "I have set you this task to train you for colour. Do you think the choice you have made will do for the purpose? Get a bunch of flowers all white." Oudry did as he was bid, and was then told to observe that the flowers are brown on the shadow side, that on a light ground they appear in half tones, and that the whitest of them are darker than absolute white. Largillière then pointed out to him the action of reflections, and made him paint by the side of the flowers various[22] white objects of different value for comparison. Oudry was not a little surprised at discovering that the flowers consisted of an accumulation of broken tones, and were given form and relief by the magic of shadows. Both Oudry and Desportes did not consider common objects unworthy of their attention, and in this way led up to the type of work in which Chardin afterwards achieved his triumphs.

PLATE III.—L'ENFANT AU TOTON (THE CHILD WITH THE TOP)
(In the Louvre)

"L'Enfant au Toton" ("The Child with the Top") is the portrait of Auguste Gabriel Godefroy, son of the jeweller Godefroy, and is the companion picture to the "Young Man with the Violin," which represents the child's elder brother Charles. The two pictures were bought in 1907 for the Louvre, at the high price of 350,000 francs. "L'Enfant au Toton" was first exhibited at the Salon of 1738, and was engraved by Lépicié in 1742. A replica of the picture was in the collection of the late M. Groult. It is one of Chardin's most delightful presentments of innocent childish amusement, and illustrates at the same time the master's supreme skill in the painting of still-life.

Chardin's still-life pictures never appear to be grouped to form balanced arrangements of line and colour. The manner how the objects are seen in the accidental position

6

in which they were left by the hands that used them holds more than a suggestion of genre painting. Indeed, it may be said that all Chardin's still-life partakes of genre as much as his genre partakes of still-life. A loaf of bread, a knife, and a black bottle on a crumpled piece of paper; a basket, a few eggs, and a copper pot, and such like material, suffice for him to create so vivid a picture of [24]simple home life, that only the presence of the housewife or serving-maid is needed to raise the painting into the sphere of domestic genre. Sometimes this scarcely needed touch of actual life is given by the introduction of some domestic animal; and in these cases we already find a hint of that unity of conception which in Chardin's genre pieces links the living creature to the surrounding inanimate objects. Take the famous "Skate" at the Louvre. On a table you see an earthen pot, a saucepan, a kettle, and a knife, grouped in accidental disorder on a negligently spread white napkin on the right; on the left are some fish and oysters and leeks, and from the wall behind is suspended a huge skate. A cat is carefully feeling its way among the oyster-shells, deeply interested in the various victuals which it eyes with eager longing. Even more pronounced is this attitude of interest in Baron Henri de Rothschild's "Chat aux Aguets." Here a crouching cat, half puzzled, half excited, is seen in[26] the extreme left corner, crouching in readiness to spring at a dead hare that is lying between a partridge and a magnificent silver tureen, and is obviously the object of the feline's hesitating attention.

It is this complete absorption of the protagonists of Chardin's genre scenes in their occupations or thoughts that fills his work with such profound human interest. Chardin is never anecdotal, never sentimental—in this respect, as well as in the solidity of his technique, and in his scientific search for colour values and atmosphere, he is vastly superior to Greuze, whose genre scenes are never free from literary flavour and from a certain kind of affectation. Nor does Chardin ever fancy himself in the rôle of the moralist like our own Hogarth, with whom he has otherwise so much in common. He looks upon his simple fellow-creatures with a sympathetic eye, watching them in the pursuit of their daily avocation, the women conscientiously following the routine of their housework or tenderly occupied[27] with the education of their children, the children themselves intent upon work or play—never posing for artistic effect, but wholly oblivious of the painter's watching eye. Chardin was by no means the first of his country's masters to devote himself to contemporary life. Just as Oudry took the first hesitating steps towards the Chardinesque conception of still-life, so Jean Raoux busied himself in the closing days of the seventeenth century with creating records of scenes taken from the daily life of the people, but he never rid himself of the sugary affected manner that was the taste of his time. It was left to Chardin to introduce into the art of genre painting in France the sense of intimacy, the homogeneous vision, the atmosphere of reality which we find in such masterpieces as the "Grace before Meat," "The Reading Lesson," "The Governess," "The Convalescent's Meal," "The Card Castle," the "Récureuse," the "Pourvoyeuse," and the famous "Child with the Top," which, after[28] having changed hands in 1845, at the time when Chardin was held in slight esteem, for less than £25, was recently bought for the Louvre, together with the companion portrait of Charles Godefroy, "The Young Man with the Violin," for the enormous price of £14,000.

In the case of each of these pictures the first thing that strikes your attention is the complete absorption of the personages in their occupation. In the picture of the boy building the card castle you can literally see him drawing in his breath for fear of upsetting the fragile structure which he is erecting. You imagine you can hear the sigh of relief with which the "Pourvoyeuse"—the woman returning from market—deposits her heavy load of bread on the dresser, whilst the sudden release of the weight that had been supported by her left arm seems to increase the strain on her right. How admirable is the expression of keen attention on the puckered brow of the child who in "The Reading Lesson"[29] tries to follow with plump finger the line indicated by the school-mistress; or the solicitude of the governess who, whilst addressing some final words of advice or admonition to the neatly dressed boy about to depart for school, has just for the moment ceased brushing his three-cornered hat. There is no need to give further instances. In all Chardin's subject pictures he opens a door upon the home life of the simple bourgeoisie to which he himself belonged by birth and character, and allows you to watch from some safe hiding-place the doings of these good folk who are utterly unaware of your presence.

Having devoted his early years to still-life, and his prime to domestic genre, Chardin lived long enough to weary his public and critics, and to find himself in the position of a fallen favourite. But though his eyesight had become affected, and his hands had lost the sureness of their touch, so that he had practically to give up oil-painting, he entered in his last years upon[30] a short career of glorious achievement in an entirely new sphere—he devoted himself to portraiture in pastel, and gained once more the enthusiastic applause of the people, even though the critics continued to exercise their severe and prejudiced judgment, and to blame him for that very verve and violence of technique which later received the Goncourt brothers' unstinted praise. "What surprising images. What violent and inspired work; what scrumbling and modelling; what rapid strokes and scratches!" His pastel portraits of himself and of his second wife, and his magnificent head of a jockey have the richness and plastic life of oil-paintings, and have indeed more boldness and virility than the work even of the most renowned of all French pastellists, La Tour. In view of their freshness and vigour, it is difficult to realise that they are the work of a suffering septuagenarian.

The mention of the hostility shown by Chardin's contemporary critics towards the system of juxtaposing touches of different[31] colour in his pastels, opens up a very interesting question with regard to the master's

9

technique of oil-painting and of the eighteenth-century critics' attitude towards it. There is no need to dwell upon the comment of a man like Mariette, who discovers in Chardin's paintings the signs of too much labour, and deplores the "heavy monotonous touch, the lack of ease in the brushwork, and the coldness of his work"—the "coldness" of the master who, alone among all the painters of his time and country, knew how to fill his canvases with a luscious warm atmosphere, and to blend his tones in the mellowest of harmonies! "His colour is not true enough," runs another of Mariette's comments.

PLATE IV.—LE BÉNÉDICITÉ (GRACE BEFORE MEAT)
(In the Louvre)

"Le Bénédicité," or "Grace before Meat," is perhaps the most popular and best known of all Chardin's domestic genre pieces. It combines the highest technical and artistic qualities with a touching simplicity of sentiment that must endear it even to those who cannot appreciate its artistry. Several replicas of it are known, but the original is probably the version in the Hermitage Collection at St. Petersburg. The Louvre owns two examples—one from the collection of Louis XV., another from the La Caze Collection. This latter version appeared three times in the Paris sale-rooms, the last time in 1876, when it realised the sum of £20! Another authentic replica is in the Marcille Collection, and yet another at Stockholm.

Let us now listen to Diderot, though in fairness it should be stated that the remarks which follow refer to Chardin's later work between 1761 and 1767. First of all he is set down as "ever a faithful imitator of Nature in his own manner, which is rude and abrupt—a nature low, common, and[32] domestic." A strange pronouncement on the part of the same ill-balanced critic who, four years later, condemned Boucher because "in all this numberless family you will not find one employed in a real act of life, studying his lesson, reading, writing, stripping hemp." Thus Chardin's vice is turned into virtue when it is a question of abusing a master who avoided the "low, common, and domestic." In his topical criticism on the Salon of 1761 Diderot tells us of Chardin, that it is long since he has "finished" anything; that he shirks trouble, and works like a man of the world who is endowed with talent and skill. In 1765 Diderot utters the following curious statement: "Chardin's technique is strange. When you are near you cannot distinguish anything; but as you step back the objects take form and begin to be real nature." On a later occasion he describes Chardin's style as "a harsh method of painting with the thumb as much as with the brush; a juxtaposition of touches, a confused and [34]sparkling accumulation of pasty and rich colours." Diderot is borne out by Bachaumont who at the same period writes: "His method is irregular. He places his colours one after the other, almost without mixing, so that his work bears a certain resemblance to mosaic, or *point carré* needlework." This description, given by two independent contemporaries, almost suggests the technique of the modern impressionists and pointillists; and if the present appearance of Chardin's paintings scarcely tallies with Diderot's and Bachaumont's explanation, it should not be forgotten that a century and a half have passed over these erstwhile "rude and violent" mosaics of colour touches, and that this stretch of time is quite sufficient to allow the colours to re-act upon each other—in a chemical sense, to permeate each other, to fuse and blend, and to form a mellow, warm, harmonious surface that shows no trace of harsh and abrupt touches. Thus it would appear that Chardin discounted the effects of time and worked for[36] posterity. In one of his rare happy moments Diderot realised this fact, and took up the cudgels for our master. In his critique of the 1767 Salon he explains that "Chardin sees his works twelve years hence; and those who condemn him are as wrong as those young artists who copy servilely at Rome the pictures painted 150 years ago."

II

Chardin's physical appearance, such as we find it in authentic portraits, his character, as it is revealed to us by his words and his actions, and the whole quiet and comparatively uneventful course of his life, are in most absolute harmony with his art. Indeed, Chardin's personality might, with a little imagination, be reconstructed from his pictures. He was a bourgeois to the finger-tips—a righteous, kind-hearted, hard-working man who never knew the consuming fire of a great passion, and who was[37] apparently free from the vagaries, inconsistencies, and irregularities usually associated with the artistic temperament. Though never overburdened with the weight of worldly possessions, he was never in real poverty, never felt the pangs of hunger. He had as good an education as his father's humble condition would permit, and his choice of a career not only met with no opposition, but was warmly encouraged. In his profession he rose slowly and gradually to high honour, and never experienced serious rebuffs or checks. His disposition was not of the kind to kindle enmity or even jealousy. His early affection for the girl who was to become his first wife was faithful, but not of the kind to prompt him to hasty action—he waited until his financial position enabled him to keep a modest home, and then he married. He married a second time, nine years after his first wife's death, and this time his choice fell upon a widow with a small fortune, a practical shrewd woman, who was of no[38] little help to him in the management of his affairs. It was not exactly a love match, but the two simple people suited each other, were of the same social position, and in similar comfortable circumstances, and managed to live peacefully and contentedly in modest bourgeois fashion.

How dull, how bald, how negative the smooth course of this life of virtue and honest labour seems, contrasted with the eventful, stormy, passionate life of a Boucher or a Fragonard who were in the stream of fashion, and adopted the manner and licentiousness and vices of their courtly patrons. There is never an immodest thought, never a piquant suggestion in Chardin's paintings. They reflect his own life; perhaps they represent the very surroundings in which he spent his busy days, for we find in their sequence the clear indication of growing prosperity from a condition which verges on poverty—respectable, not sordid, poverty—to comparative luxury; from drudgery in kitchen and courtyard to [40]tea in the cosy parlour. There can be but little doubt that many a time the master's brush was devoted to the recording of his own home, his own family, the even tenor of his life.

PLATE V.—LA GOUVERNANTE (MOTHER AND SON)
(In the collection of Prince Liechtenstein in Vienna)

"La Gouvernante," or "Mother and Son," is one of the most attractive of the many Chardin pictures in the collection of Prince Liechtenstein in Vienna. Observe the perfectly natural attitude of the woman and the child, in which there is not the slightest hint of posing for the artist. Like all Chardin's genre pictures, it is, as it were, a glimpse of real life. This picture and its companion "La Mère Laborieuse" figured at the sale of Chardin's works after his death, when his art received such scant appreciation that the pair only realised 30 livres 4 sous!

The man's character—and more than that, his *milieu*—are expressed in no uncertain fashion in his three auto-portraits, two of which are at the Louvre, and one in the Collection of M. Léon Michel-Lévy. A good, kind-hearted, simple-minded man he appears in these pastel portraits, which all date from the last years of his life, a man incapable of wickedness or meanness, and endowed with a keen sense of humour that lingers about the corners of his

13

mouth. It is a face that immediately enlists sympathy by its obvious readiness for sympathy with others. And so convincing are these portraits in their straightforward bold statement, that they may be accepted as documentary testimony to the man's character, even if we had not the evidence of Fragonard's much earlier portrait of Chardin,[42] which was until recently in the Rodolphe Kann Collection, and is at present in the possession of Messrs. Duveen Bros. With the exception of such differences as may be accounted for by the differences of age, all these portraits tally to a remarkable degree. The features are the same, and the expression is identical—the same keen, penetrating eyes, which even in his declining years have lost none of their searching intelligence, even though they have to be aided by round horn-rimmed spectacles; the same revelation of a lovable nature, even though in M. Michel-Lévy's version worry and suffering have left their traces on the features. He is the embodiment of decent middle-class respectability. Decency and a high sense of honour marked every act of his life, and decency had to be kept up in external appearances. On his very deathbed, when he was tortured by the pangs of one of the most terrible of diseases, dropsy having set in upon stone, he still insisted upon his daily shave!

[43]Yet Chardin, the bourgeois incarnate, was anything but a Philistine. From this he was saved by his life-long devotion to, and his ardent enthusiasm for, his art. He was not given to bursts of the theatrical eloquence that is so dear to the men of his race; but the scanty records we have of his sayings testify to the humble, profound respect in which he held the art of painting. "Art is an island of which I have only skirted the coast-line," runs the often quoted phrase to which he gave utterance at a time when he had attained to his highest achievement. To an artist who talked to him about his method of improving the colours, he replied in characteristic fashion: "And who has told you, sir, that one paints with colours?" "With what then?"

questioned his perplexed interviewer. "One *uses* colours, but one paints with feeling."

Brilliant technician as he was, and admirable critic of his own and other artists' work, Chardin lacked the gift to communicate his knowledge to others. He was[44] a bad teacher—he was a wretched teacher. Even such pliable material as Fragonard's genius yielded no results to his honest efforts. It was Boucher who, at the height of his vogue and overburdened with commissions that did not allow him the time to devote himself to the nursing of a raw talent, recommended Fragonard to work in Chardin's studio; but six months' teaching by the master failed to bring out the pupil's brilliant gifts. Chardin knew not how to impart his marvellous technique to young Fragonard, and Fragonard returned to Boucher without having appreciably benefited by Chardin's instruction. The master had no better luck with his own son, though in this case the failure was due rather to lack of talent than to bad teaching, for Van Loo and Natoire were equally unsuccessful in their efforts to develop the unfortunate young man's feeble gifts. There is a touch of deepest pathos in the reference made by Chardin to his son at the close of an address to his Academic colleagues in 1765:[45] "Gentlemen, gentlemen, be indulgent! He who has not felt the difficulty of art does nothing that counts; he who, like my son, has felt it too much, does nothing at all. Farewell, gentlemen, and be indulgent, be indulgent!"

Chardin had no artistic progeny to carry on his tradition, partly, perhaps, because he failed as a teacher, more probably because the Revolution and the Empire were close at hand when he died, and because the social upheavals led to new ideals and to an art that was based on an altogether different æsthetic code. The star of David rose when Chardin's gave its last flickers; and Chardin himself was among the commissioners who signed on the 10th of January 1778 the highly laudatory report on David's large battle sketch sent to Paris by the Director of the School of Rome. Yet who would venture to-day to mention the two in the same breath. David has fallen into well-deserved oblivion, and the example of Chardin's glorious paintings has done what[46] was beyond the master's own power—it has created a School that is daily enlisting an increasing number of highly gifted followers. Chardin's name is honoured and revered in every modern painter's studio.

III

Jean-Baptiste Siméon Chardin was born in Paris on November 2, 1699, the second son of Jean Chardin, cabinetmaker, or to be more strict, billiard-table maker, a hard-working man who rose to be syndic of his corporation, but who, the father of a family of five, was fortunately not sufficiently prosperous to give his son a literary education. I say fortunately, because it was probably his ignorance of mythology and classic lore that made Chardin, who often bitterly regretted his educational deficiencies, turn his attention to those subjects which required a keenly observing eye and a sure hand, and not a fertile imagination stimulated[47] by book-knowledge. His lack of education saved Chardin from allegorical and mythological clap-trap, and made him the great painter of the visible world of his time. Though Jean Chardin wanted his son to take up his own profession, he was quick in recognising and encouraging the boy's early talent, and finally made him enter the Atelier of Pierre Jacques Cazes where Siméon received his first systematic training. Cazes was a capable enough painter in the traditional grand manner of Le Brun, which had been taught to him by Bon Boullogne. He had taken the Prix de Rome, and issued victorious from several other competitions, but, like Rigaud and Largillière and several other distinguished painters of the period, never availed himself of the privilege entailed by the award of the Prix de Rome. Indeed, he was not a little proud of this fact, as he showed by his reply to Crozat who commiserated with him for having never seen the Italian masterpieces—"I have proved that one can do without them." Yet whatever[48] merit there may have been in Cazes' work, and whatever may have been his own opinion on this subject, prosperity came not his way; and although he was appointed Professor at the Academy, and rose to great popularity as a teacher, he remained so poor that he could not afford to provide his pupils with living models. They had to learn what they could from copying their master's compositions and studies.

The copying of designs, based on literary conceptions and knowledge of the classics, could not possibly be either beneficial or attractive for a youth who lacked the education needed for understanding these subjects, and who was, moreover, deeply interested in the life that came under his personal observation. The tasks set to him by Cazes must have appeared to Chardin like the drudgery of acquiring proficiency in a hieroglyphic language that conveyed no definite meaning to him. Still, Chardin made such progress under his first master that Noël Nicolas Coypel engaged [50]him as assistant to paint the details in some decorative over-door panels representing the Seasons and the Pleasures of the Chase.

PLATE VI.—LA MÈRE LABORIEUSE
(In the Stockholm Museum)

"La Mère Laborieuse," which is the companion picture to "La Gouvernante," was first exhibited at the Salon of 1745, where it attracted the attention of Count Tessin, who immediately commissioned the replica which is now at the Stockholm Museum. The picture was engraved by Lépicié in the same year in which it was first exhibited.

In Coypel Chardin found a master of very different calibre—a teacher after his own heart. The systematised knowledge of the principles adopted by the late Bolognese masters, rules of composition and of the distribution of light and shade, were certainly of little use to him when, on beginning his work in Coypel's studio, he was set the task of painting a gun in the hand of a sportsman. Chardin was

17

amazed at the trouble taken by his employer, and at the amount of thought expended by him upon the placing and lighting of the object. The painting of this gun was Chardin's first valuable lesson. He was made to realise the importance of a comparatively insignificant accessory. He was shown how its position would affect the rhythm of the design. He was taught to paint with minute accuracy whatever his eye beheld. He was[52] told, perhaps for the first time, that it was not enough to paint a hieroglyphic that will be recognised to represent a gun, but that the paint should express the true appearance of the object, its plastic form, its surface, the texture of the material, the play of light and shade and reflections. The lesson of this gun gave the death blow to traditional recipes, and laid the foundation of Chardin's art.

Chardin did well under the new tuition, so well that Jean-Baptiste Van Loo engaged him to help in the restoration of some paintings in the gallery of Fontainebleau. It must have been a formidable task, since not only Chardin, but J. B. Van Loo's younger brother Charles and some Academy students were made to join the master's staff. Five francs a day and an excellent dinner on the completion of the work were the wages for the job which in some way was a memorable event in our master's life. With the exception of a visit to Rouen in his old age, the trip to Fontainebleau[53] afforded Chardin the only glimpse he ever had of the world beyond Paris and the surrounding district.

The first record we have of Chardin's independent activity has reference to an astonishing piece of work which has disappeared long since, but is known to us from an etching by J. de Goncourt. The work in question was a large signboard, 14 feet 3 inches long by 2 feet 3 inches wide, commissioned from him by a surgeon who was on terms of friendship with Chardin's father. Perhaps the young artist had seen Watteau's famous signboard for Gersaint, now in the German Emperor's Collection. However this may be, like Watteau he departed from the customary practice of filling the board with a design made up of the implements of the patron's craft,1 and painted an animated street scene, representing the sequel to a duel. The scene is [54]outside the house of a surgeon who is attending to the wound of the defeated combatant, whilst a group of idle folk of all conditions, attracted by curiosity, have assembled in the street, and are watching the proceedings, and excitedly discussing the occurrence. Although Goncourt's etching naturally gives no indication of the colour and technique of this remarkable and unconventional painting, it enables us to see the very natural and skilful grouping and the excellent management of light and shade which Chardin had mastered even at that early period.

The sign was put up on a Sunday, and attracted a vast crowd whose exclamations induced the surgeon to step outside his house and ascertain the cause of the stir. Being a man of little taste, his anger was aroused by Chardin's bold departure from convention, but the general approval with which the *quartier* greeted Chardin's original conception soon soothed his ruffled spirit, and the incident led to no further unpleasantness.

[55]Save for the story of the surgeon's sign, nothing is known of Chardin's doings from his days of apprenticeship to his first appearance, in 1728, at the *Exposition de la Jeunesse*, a kind of open-air Salon without jury, held annually in the Place Dauphine on Corpus Christi day, between 6 A.M. and midday, "weather permitting." With the exception of the annual Salon at the Louvre, which was only open to the works of the members of the Academy, this *Exposition de la Jeunesse* was the only opportunity given to artists for submitting their works to the public. At the time when Chardin made his début at this picture fair, the annual Academy Salon instituted by Louis XIV. had been abandoned for some years, so that even the members of the Academy were driven to the Place Dauphine in order to keep in touch with the public. In the contemporary criticisms of the *Mercure* the names of all the greatest French masters of the first half of the eighteenth century are to

19

be [56] found among the exhibitors of the *Jeunesse*—the shining lights of the profession, Coypel, Rigaud, De Troy, among the crowd of youngsters eager to make their reputation. Lancret, Oudry, Boucher, Nattier, Lemoine—none of them disdained to show their works under conditions which had much more in common with those that obtain at an annual fair, than with those we are accustomed to associate with a picture exhibition. The spectacle of dignified Academicians thus seeking public suffrage in the street finally induced Louis de Boullogne, Director of the Academy, to seek for an amelioration of the prevailing conditions, and thanks to the intervention of the Comptroller-general of the King's Buildings the Salon of the Louvre was re-opened in 1725 for a term of four days—"outsiders" being excluded as of yore.

On Corpus Christi day, 1728, Chardin, then in his twenty-ninth year, availed himself for the first time of the opportunity given to rising talent, and made his appearance at [57] the Place Dauphine with a dozen still-life paintings, including "The Skate" and "The Buffet"—the two masterpieces which are counted to-day among the treasured possessions of the Louvre. This sudden revelation of so personal and fully developed a talent caused no little stir. Chardin was hailed as a master worthy to be placed beside the great Netherlandish still-life painters, and was urged by his friends to "present himself" forthwith at the Academy. Chardin reluctantly followed the advice, and, having arranged his pictures ready for inspection in the first room of the Academy at the Louvre, retired to an adjoining apartment, where he awaited, not without serious misgivings, the result of his bold venture.

His fears proved to be unfounded. A contemporary of Chardin's has left an amusing account of what befell our timid artist. M. de Largillière entered the first room and carefully examined the pictures placed there by Chardin. Then he passed into the next room to speak to the candidate. [58] "You have here some very fine pictures which are surely the work of some good Flemish painter—

an excellent school for colour, this Flemish school. Now let us see your works." "Sir, you have just seen them." "What! these were your pictures?" "Yes, sir." "Then," said Largillière, "present yourself, my friend, present yourself." Cazes, Chardin's old master, likewise fell into the innocent trap, and was equally complimentary, without suspecting the authorship of the exposed pictures. In fact, he undertook to stand as his pupil's sponsor. When Louis de Boullogne, Director of the Academy and painter to the king, arrived, Chardin informed him that the exhibited pictures were painted by him, and that the Academy might dispose of those which were approved of. "He is not yet 'confirmed' (*agréé*) and he talks already of being 'received' (*reçu*)!2However," he added, "you have done well to [60]mention it." He reported the proposal, which was immediately accepted. The ballot resulted in Chardin being at the same time, "confirmed" and "received." On Sept. 25, 1728, he was sworn in, and became a full member of the Academy. In recognition of his rare genius, and in consideration of his impecunious condition, his entrance fee was reduced to 100 livres. "The Buffet" and a "Kitchen" piece were accepted as "diploma pictures."

PLATE VII.—LE PANNEAU DE PÊCHES
(In the Louvre)

"Le Panneau de Pêches," (The Basket of Peaches) is a magnificent instance of Chardin's extraordinary skill in the rendering of textures and substances. Note the perfect truth of all the colour-values, the play of light and shade and reflections, such as the opening up of the shadow thrown by the tumbler owing to the refractive qualities of the wine contained in the glass. Note, also, the "accidental" appearance of the carefully grouped objects—the manner in which the knife-handle projects from the table. The plate is reproduced from the original painting at the Louvre in Paris.

In spite of this sudden success, Chardin was by no means on the road to fortune. His pictures sold slowly and at very low prices. He always had a very modest opinion of the financial value of his works, and was ever ready to part with them at ridiculously low prices, or to offer them as presents to his friends. The story goes that on one occasion, when his friend Le Bas wished to buy a picture which Chardin was just finishing, he offered to exchange it for a pretty waistcoat. When the king's sister admired one of his pastel portraits and[62] asked the price, he immediately begged her to accept it "as a token of gratitude for her interest in his work." Admirably tactful is the form in which Chardin gives practical expression to his gratitude for M. de Vandières' successful efforts at procuring him a pension from the king. Through Lépicié, the secretary of the Academy, he begs Vandières to accept the dedication of an engraving after his "Lady with a Bird-organ"; and asks permission to state on the margin*that the original painting is in the Collection of M. de Vandières.* The request was granted.

Small wonder, then, if in spite of the modesty of his personal requirements Chardin, even after his election to the Academy, had to wait over two years before he was in a position to marry Marguerite Sainctar, whom he had met at a dance some years before, and who during the period of waiting had lost her health, her parents, and her modest fortune, and had to go to live with her guardian. Chardin's father, who had[63] warmly approved of his son's engagement, now objected to the marriage, but nothing could deter Siméon from his honourable purpose, and the marriage took place at St. Sulpice on February 1, 1731. He took his wife to his parents' house at the corner of the Rue Princesse, where he had been living before his marriage, and before the end of the year he was presented with a son, who was given the name Pierre Jean-Baptiste. Two years later a daughter was born—Marguerite Agnes; but Chardin's domestic happiness was not destined to last long, for on April 14, 1735, he lost both wife and daughter.

His son was, however, his greatest source of grief. Remembering the imaginary disadvantages he had suffered from his lack of humanistic education, he determined that his boy should be better equipped for the artistic profession, and had him thoroughly well instructed in the classics. He then had him prepared at one of the Academy ateliers for competing for the Prix de Rome.[64] No doubt owing to his father's then rather powerful influence, Pierre Chardin gained the coveted prize in 1754, and after having passed his three years' probation at the recently established *École des élèves protégés*, which he had entered with the second batch of pupils by whom the first successful "Romans" were replaced, he set out for Rome in October 1757. But Pierre, discouraged perhaps from his earliest attempts by the perfection of his father's art which he could never hope to attain, indolent moreover and intractable, made little progress under Natoire, who was then Director of the School of Rome. Pierre worked little, quarrelled with his colleagues, and never produced either a copy or an original work that was considered good enough to be sent to Paris. "He does not know how to handle the brush, and what he does looks like a tired and not very pleasing attempt," runs Natoire's report to Marigny in 1761. He returned to Paris in 1762, but his whole life was a failure. He fully realised his[65] inability ever to arrive at artistic achievement. In 1767 he went to Venice with the French ambassador, the Marquis de Paulmy, and was never heard of since. It was said that he had found his death in the waters of a Venetian Canal.

But to return to Siméon Chardin—we find him again among the exhibitors of the Place Dauphine in 1732, with some pieces of still-life, two large decorative panels of musical trophies, and a wonderfully realistic painting in imitation of a bronze bas-relief after a terra-cotta of Duquesnoy. These imitation reliefs were then much in vogue for over-doors and wall decorations in the houses of the great, as, for instance, in the Palace of Compiègne. Two authentic pieces of the kind, executed in grisaille, are in the

Collection of Dr. Tuffier. The one of the 1732 exhibition was bought by Van Loo for 200 livres, and is now in the Marcille Collection. According to contemporary criticism the bronze-tone of the relief was so perfectly rendered that it|66| produced an illusion "which touch alone can destroy."

About this time Chardin's still-life period comes to a close, and we find him henceforth devoting the best of his power to the domestic genre "à la Teniers" (as it was dubbed by his own patrons and contemporaries), though even in later years still-life pieces continue to figure now and then among his Salon exhibits. His first triumphs in the new field of action were scored in 1734, when his sixteen contributions to the *Jeunesse* exhibition included the "Washerwoman" (now in the Hermitage Collection), the "Woman drawing Water" (painted in several versions or replicas, of which the best known are at the Stockholm Museum, and in the Collections of Sir Frederick Cook at Richmond and of M. Eudoxe Marcille in Paris); the "Card Castle" (now in the Collection of Baron Henri de Rothschild); and the "Lady sealing a Letter" (in the German Emperor's Collection). It is interesting to note that this last named picture is the|67| only genre piece by Chardin with life size figures.

Chardin's new departure immediately found favour, and although he continued to charge ludicrously inadequate prices for his work, which, with the deliberate slowness of his method, prevented him from rising to well deserved prosperity, he not only experienced no difficulty in disposing of his pictures, but had to duplicate and reduplicate them to meet the demand of his patrons, foremost among whom were the Swedish Count Tessin and the Austrian Prince Liechtenstein. In view of the many versions that exist of most of the master's genre pieces it is often difficult or impossible to decide which is the original, and which a replica. The artist's modesty with regard to his charges may be gathered from the fact that, at the time of his highest vogue, he only asked twenty-five louis-d'or a piece for two pictures commissioned by Count Tessin, whilst the painter Wille was able to secure a pair for thirty-six livres.

[68]Three of the genre pictures of the 1734 exhibition were sent by Chardin in the following year to a competitive show held by the Academicians to fill the vacancies of professor, adjuncts, and councillors of the Academy; but Chardin was among the unsuccessful candidates, the votes declaring in favour of Michel and Carle Van Loo, Boucher, Natoire, Lancret, and Parrocel.

The regular course of the Academy Salons, which had been interrupted since 1704, save for the tentative four days' exhibition at the Louvre in 1725, was resumed in 1737, first in alternate years, and then annually without break until the present day. At the inaugural exhibition Chardin exhibited again the three pieces of the 1732 and 1735 shows, together with Van Loo's bronze relief, the portrait of his friend Aved (known as "Le Souffleur," or "The Chemist"), and several pictures of children playing, a class of subject in which the master stands unrivalled among the Frenchmen of his time. Fragonard, of [70]course, achieved greatness as a painter of children, but to him the child was an object for portraiture, whilst Chardin, the student of life, painted the *life*, the work and pleasures, of the child, at the same time never losing sight of portraiture.

PLATE VIII.—LA POURVOYEUSE
(In the Louvre)

"La Pourvoyeuse," of which picture the first dated version, painted in 1738, is in the possession of the German Emperor, is one of the most masterly of Chardin's earlier pictures of homely incidents of everyday life. The attitude of the woman, who has just returned from market and is depositing her load of victuals, is admirably true to life; and the still-life painting of the black bottles on the ground, the pewter plate, the loaf of bread, and so forth, testifies to the master's supreme skill. From the glimpse of the courtyard through the open door, it can be seen that

25

the setting of the sun is identical with that of "The Fountain"—that is to say, that it represents the modest house in the Rue Princesse, in which Chardin lived up to the time of his second marriage. Another replica is in the collection of Prince Liechtenstein in Vienna. Our plate is reproduced from the version in the Louvre.

His success was decisive. His reputation was now firmly established, and still further increased by his next year's exhibit of eight pictures—among them the "Boy with the Top," and also the "Lady sealing a Letter," which he had already shown at the Jeunesse exhibition in 1734. Six pictures followed in the next year, including the "Governess," the "Pourvoyeuse" (now in the Louvre), and the "Cup of Tea"; and in 1740 his popularity reached its zenith with the exhibition of his masterpiece "Grace before Meat" (*le Bénédicité*), in addition to which he showed the two *singeries*—"The Monkey Painter" and "The Monkey Antiquary" (now in the Louvre)—even Chardin could not hold out against the bad taste which applauded this stupid invention[72] of the Netherlanders—and several other domestic genre pieces. A replica of the Bénédicité was commissioned by Count Tessin for the King of Sweden, and is now at the Stockholm Museum.

The bad state of his health seriously interfered with his work during the next few years, and his contributions to the Salon of 1741 were restricted to "The Morning Toilet" and "M. Lenoir's Son building a Card Castle," whilst he was an absentee from the following year's exhibition.

In 1743 Chardin lost his mother, with whom he had been living since his wife's death, and who had been looking after his boy's early education. Chardin, slow worker as he always was, and overwhelmed with commissions for new pictures and replicas, which he continued to paint at starvation rates, had no time to devote to the bringing up of his son, which was perhaps one of the reasons which induced him to marry, in the year following his mother's death, a musketeer's widow, of thirty-seven, Fran[73]çoise Marguerite Pouget, a worthy woman of no particular personal charm, to judge from the portrait left by the master's chalks, but an excellent housekeeper who managed to bring a certain degree of order into her husband's affairs, and proved to be of no little assistance to him in his business dealings. It was not exactly a love match, but there is no reason for doubting that the two worthy people lived in complete harmony and enjoyed a fair amount of comfort. The repeated references to his "financial troubles" need not be taken in too literal a sense, since from 1744, the year of his marriage, when he transferred his quarters to his wife's house in the Rue Princesse, until 1774, when his affairs really took a turn for the bad, he enjoyed the ownership of a house which he was then able to sell for 18,000 livres, a by no means paltry amount for these days. Moreover, in 1752, Lépicié's endeavours resulted in the grant of a pension of 500 livres by the king, which, according to the petitioner's own[74] words, was sufficient to secure Chardin's comfort. True enough, when the artist died in 1779, his widow applied for relief on the pretext of being practically left without means of subsistence. But an investigation of the case led to the discovery that she was in enjoyment of an annual income of from 6000 to 8000 livres! A daughter, who was born to the master by his second wife, died soon after having seen the light of the world.

The year 1746 was apparently more productive than the five preceding years; but henceforth the number of his subject pictures became more and more restricted, and Chardin, perhaps discouraged by the public grumbling at his lack of original invention, returned to the sphere of his early successes—to still-life. Meanwhile his probity and uprightness had gained him the highest esteem of his Academic colleagues and brought him new honours in his official position. He was appointed Treasurer of the Academy in 1755, and soon afterwards[75] succeeded J. A. Portail as "hanger" of the Salon exhibition, a difficult office which needed a man of Chardin's tact, fairness, and honesty.

When Chardin took up his duties as Treasurer he found the finances of the Academy in a deplorable condition. His predecessor J. B. Reydellet, who had acted as "huissier and concierge," had neither been able to exercise a restraining influence upon the rowdy tendencies of the students, nor to keep even a semblance of order in the accounts. On his death his legacy to the Academy was a deficit of close on 10,000 livres. Chardin, assisted by his business-like wife, did his best to wipe off the effects of his predecessor's negligence or incompetence, but the task added very considerably to his worries, especially as, owing to financial stress, the Academicians' pensions were frequently kept in arrear, and for years Royal support was withheld. Matters reached a climax in 1772, when the Academy found itself in such straits,[76] that the question of dissolving the institution had to be seriously considered. Chardin's appeal to Marigny, and through him to the Abbé Terray, Comptroller-General of Finances, however, led to the desired result, and the much needed support was granted.

The quarters at the Louvre, vacated by the death of the king's engraver and goldsmith Marteau in March 1757, were given to Chardin, who let his house in the Rue Princesse to Joseph Vernet—another change which must have contributed considerably to the ageing master's peace of mind. In his wonted slow manner he continued to paint still-life, and received several important commissions for the decoration of Royal and other residences. Thus, in 1764, his friend Cochin procured for him, through Marigny, a commission for some over-doors for the Château of Choisy. They depicted the attributes of Science, Art, and Music, and were exhibited in the Salon of 1765. A similar order for two over-doors[77] in the music-room of the Château of Bellevue—the instruments of civil and of military music—followed in the next year. The payment for the five, which was delayed until 1771, amounted to 5000 livres.

Chardin's last years were saddened by the tragic end of his son and by a terribly painful illness. His duties as Treasurer became too much for him, and he resigned this office to the sculptor Coustou in 1774. There was a small deficit which he volunteered to make good, but this offer was declined, and a banquet was given to him by his colleagues as an expression of their appreciation of his services. The acute suffering caused by his illness did not prevent him from continuing his artistic work, and we find him at the very end of his career branching out in an entirely new direction. The pastel portraits of his closing years betray no decline in keenness of vision and in power of expression. Indeed, they must be counted among his finest achievements. He worked to the very last,[78] and sent some pastel heads to the Salon of 1779. On the 6th of December of the same year he breathed his last. His remains were buried at St. Germain-l'Auxerrois, in the parish of the Louvre. With him died the art of the French eighteenth century. A kind fate had saved him from the misfortune that fell to the share of his contemporaries Fragonard and Greuze, who outlived him by many years, but who also outlived the *ancien régime* and died in poverty and neglect and misery.

The plates are printed by BEMROSE & SONS, LTD.,
London and Derby
The text at the BALLANTYNE PRESS, Edinburgh

Footnotes

1 A signboard of the conventional type, but painted with all Chardin's consummate mastery, is the one executed for the perfume distiller Pinaud, which appeared at the Guildhall Exhibition in 1902, and at Whitechapel in 1907.

2 The candidates had to pass through a probationary stage before they were definitely received by the Academy.

61892597R00020